Cock-a-Doodle-Doo!
A Day on the Farm

Cock-a-Doodle-Doo!
A Day on the Farm

Venice Shone

Cartwheel
·B·O·O·K·S· TM

SCHOLASTIC INC.
New York   Toronto   London   Auckland   Sydney

For Danny

Originally published in Great Britain by Orchard Books, London.

Copyright © 1991 by Venice Shone.
All rights reserved. First published in the U.S.A. by Scholastic Inc., by arrangement with Orchard Books. Published simultaneously in Canada.
CARTWHEEL BOOKS is a trademark of Scholastic Inc.

LIBRARY OF CONGRESS CATALOGING-IN-PUBLICATION DATA
Shone, Venice.
　　Cock-a-doodle-doo! : a day on the farm / Venice Shone.
　　　　p.　cm.
　　"Cartwheel books."
　　Summary: The animal inhabitants of a farm enjoy their day, from sunrise to the fall of darkness.
　　ISBN 0-590-45425-0
　　[1. Domestic animals—Fiction.]　I. Title.
PZ7.S55865Co　1992
[E]—dc20
91-24667
CIP
AC

12 11 10 9 8 7 6 5 4 3 2 1　　　　2 3 4 5 6 7/9

Printed in Belgium

First Scholastic printing, March 1992

Cock-a-doodle-doo!
The rooster is crowing.
The day is beginning.

Here comes the sun,

rising over the hill.

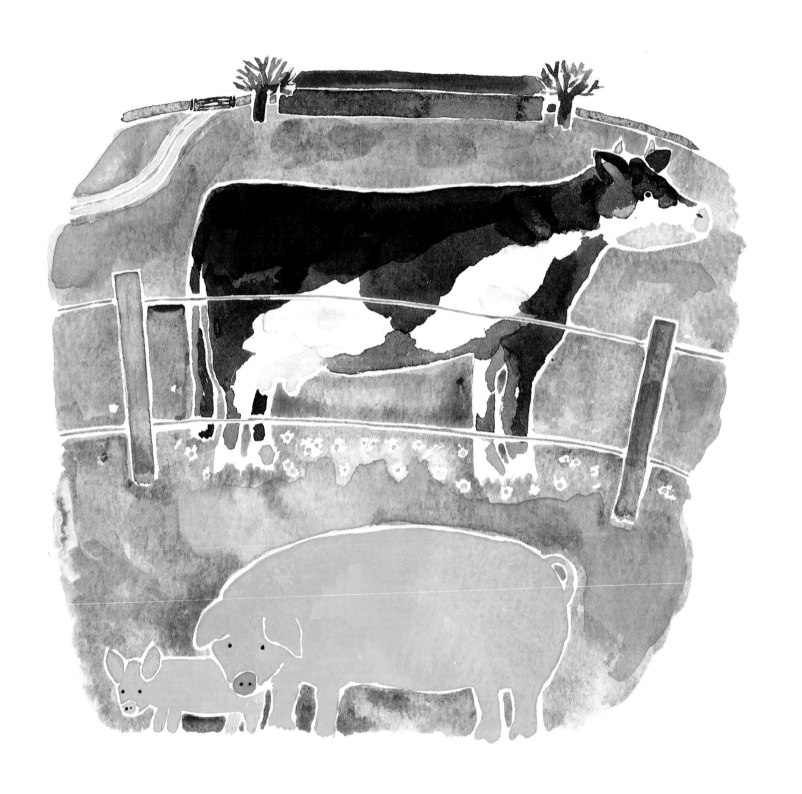

All around the farm

the animals are waking.

The cows are mooing.

It's milking time!

High on the hill

the lambs are playing.

Down in the field

the farmer is working.

Over in the orchard

the rabbits are hopping.

Close by in the yard

the hens and geese are pecking.

The goat is in the garden

where the vegetables are growing.

The pigs in their sty are

feeding and wallowing in mud.

Here comes the rain!

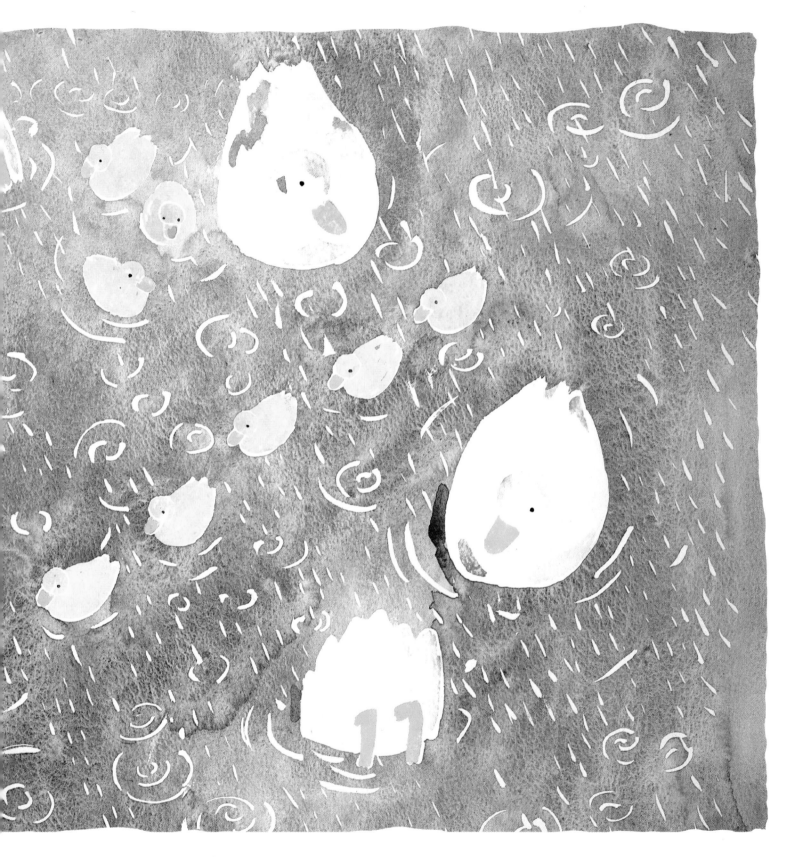

The ducks are happy splashing.

The horses in the stable

are warm and dry.

Now the day is ending.

The cows are coming home.

In the darkness outside
the owl is calling.

Too-whit-too-whoo!

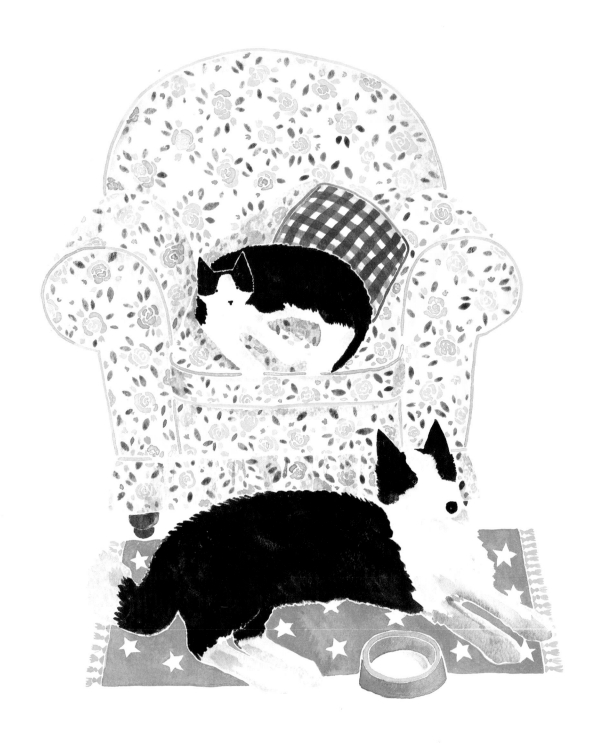

The farm cat and dog
are safe and snug inside.
Good night!